SAMURAI

KENNY ABDO

Fly!
An Imprint of Abdo Zoom
abdobooks.com

abdobooks.com

Published by Abdo Zoom, a division of ABDO, P.O. Box 398166, Minneapolis,
Minnesota 55439. Copyright © 2021 by Abdo Consulting Group, Inc. International
copyrights reserved in all countries. No part of this book may be reproduced in any
form without written permission from the publisher. Fly!™ is a trademark and logo
of Abdo Zoom.

Printed in the United States of America, North Mankato, Minnesota.
102020
012021

THIS BOOK CONTAINS
RECYCLED MATERIALS

Photo Credits: Alamy, Everett Collection, Granger Collection, iStock,
North Wind Picture Archives, Shutterstock
Production Contributors: Kenny Abdo, Jennie Forsberg, Grace Hansen
Design Contributors: Dorothy Toth, Neil Klinepier, Laura Graphenteen

Library of Congress Control Number: 2019956156

Publisher's Cataloging-in-Publication Data

Names: Abdo, Kenny, author.
Title: Samurai / by Kenny Abdo
Description: Minneapolis, Minnesota : Abdo Zoom, 2021 | Series: Ancient warriors |
    Includes online resources and index.
Identifiers: ISBN 9781098221256 (lib. bdg.) | ISBN 9781098222239 (ebook) |
    ISBN 9781098222727 (Read-to-Me ebook)
Subjects: LCSH: Samurai--Juvenile literature. | Japan--Juvenile literature. |
    Civilization, Medieval--Juvenile literature. | Military art and science--Juvenile
    literature. | Soldiers--Juvenile literature.
Classification: DDC 355.00952--dc23

TABLE OF CONTENTS

SAMURAI

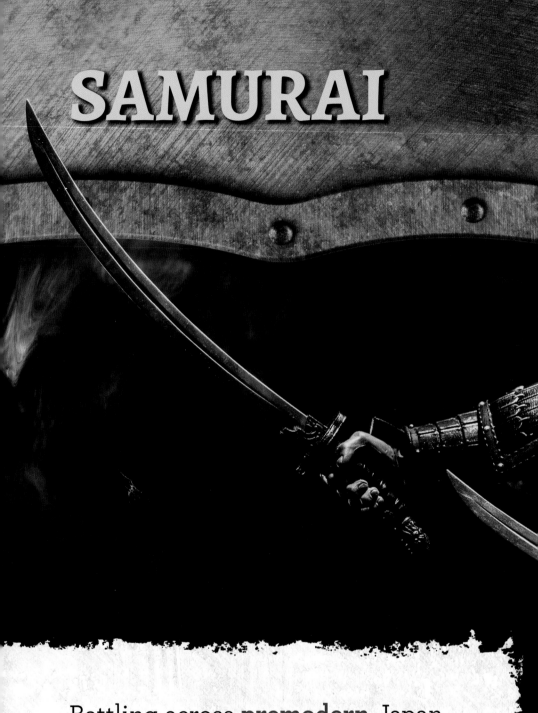

Battling across **premodern** Japan, Samurai warriors fought with honor and fierceness.

These ruthless but noble fighters lived and died by the samurai code. It is known as the *Bushidō*. It means "the way of the warrior."

THE WARRIORS

The word *samurai* means "those who serve" in Japanese.

Samurai started as **henchmen** for wealthy landowners during the **Heian Period**.

Samurai women were known as *Onna-bugeisha*. They fought alongside male samurai.

WARFARE & TACTICS

Samurai would carry two steel swords. One was a *katana*. It had a long, sharp blade. They also carried a short sword called a *tanto* used for protection. Samurai were also skilled with bows and arrows.

Samurai wore full suits of armor. It was made of thick leather. They also wore helmets that were called *kabutos*.

The difficult training of a samurai
warrior began in childhood. Samurai
school was a mix of physical training,
history studies, and **discipline**.

The Battle of Sekigahara was the greatest samurai battle of all time. Fought on October 21, 1600, it was a battle of east over west. It divided Japan into two major sides for more than 250 years.

The samurai **class** was banned by the mid-1870s. It was around then that their **privileged** status ended.

ARE YOU NOT ENTERTAINED?!

Samurai have been featured in many forms of entertainment. They have appeared in books and classic films, like Akira Kurosawa's *Seven Samurai*.

Modern Japan still maintains a culture based on the *Bushidō*. This shows that you don't have to be a warrior to live with honor.

GLOSSARY

class – a group of people who have a similar way of life and position in society.

discipline – training of the body or mind according to rules or principles.

Heian Period – an era in Japanese history between 794 CE and 1185 CE. It was named after the location of the imperial capital Heian-kyō.

henchmen – a loyal follower and helper, especially of someone engaged in unethical or criminal deeds.

premodern – the era before the modern one.

privilege – a great advantage or special right only available to a particular group of people.

ONLINE RESOURCES

Booklinks
NONFICTION NETWORK
FREE! ONLINE NONFICTION RESOURCES

To learn more about Samurai, please visit **abdobooklinks.com** or scan this QR code. These links are routinely monitored and updated to provide the most current information available.

INDEX